# Lucky
# Duck

First published in paperback in 2005
First published in 2004 by Macmillan Children's Books
A division of Macmillan Publishers Limited
20 New Wharf Road, London N1 9RR
Basingstoke and Oxford
Associated companies throughout the world
www.panmacmillan.com

ISBN 0 333 98671 7

A CIP catalogue record for this book is available from the British Library.

Printed in Belgium by Proost

# Lucky Duck

Written by
Jonathan Shipton

Illustrated by
Suzanne Diederen

MACMILLAN CHILDREN'S BOOKS

When Lenny was a very little boy, his dad bought him a really special toy duck.

Duck was Lenny's best thing and whatever Lenny did, Duck did too.

They played together.

They read together.

Even when Lenny
went to nursery,
Duck had his own
special place to sit.

So, when they went to the seaside to visit Gran, Lenny made sure there was an extra bucket and spade for Duck.

Lenny really liked playing
on the beach. So did Duck.

Sometimes they paddled together,
and sometimes they built
sandcastles with flags on top.

But one day, when it was time
to go home, somewhere in the rush
of packing and kissing goodbye,
Lenny's little duck
got lost.

When Lenny realised, well,
he had never been so
unhappy in his
whole life.

They searched the house, upside down and inside out.

They even looked
all along the beach,
but they couldn't find
Duck anywhere.

Poor Lenny had
to go all the way
home without his
duck to cuddle.

Lenny tried hard to be brave,
but he missed his duck very much.
Even though he had lots of other
lovely toys, no one was
quite as special as Duck.

Every night for a long time, Duck would appear in Lenny's dreams. And Lenny would wonder where Duck was and what he was doing.

But time passed, and Lenny
grew up. He began to
play with lots of
different toys.

And he nearly forgot about the little duck with an orange beak and bright button eyes.

Nearly . . . but not quite.

Many years later, when Lenny was a grown-up,
he had a little boy of his own, called Ben.

One summer, Lenny took Ben to visit Gran at the seaside.

It was cold and raining, and Ben was very bored.

So Lenny said, "When I was little, I always loved exploring.
Why don't you see what you can find?"

Ben crawled inside Gran's old wardrobes.

He looked underneath all the beds.

Then he found some little stairs, and climbed all the way up to the attic . . .

When Ben came
back down, he just
couldn't stop smiling.

He was holding something white and fluffy.
He held it out to show Lenny.

It was
DUCK!

His orange beak was a little bit dirty and his white fur was very dusty, but he was still the same soft, cuddly Duck.

And that's what happens with some lucky ducks.

They get lost . . .

and squashed . . .

and left behind,
but one day . . .

. . . they find their boy!